Dear Parent:

Congratulations! Your child is taking the first steps on an exciting journey. The destination? Independent reading!

STEP INTO READING® will help your child get there. The program offers books at five levels that accompany children from their first attempts at reading to reading success. Each step includes fun stories, fiction and nonfiction, and colorful art. There are also Step into Reading Sticker Books, Step into Reading Math Readers, and Step into Reading Phonics Readers— a complete literacy program with something to interest every child.

Learning to Read, Step by Step!

Ready to Read   Preschool–Kindergarten
• big type and easy words • rhyme and rhythm • picture clues
For children who know the alphabet and are eager to begin reading.

Reading with Help   Preschool–Grade 1
• basic vocabulary • short sentences • simple stories
For children who recognize familiar words and sound out new words with help.

Reading on Your Own   Grades 1–3
• engaging characters • easy-to-follow plots • popular topics
For children who are ready to read on their own.

Reading Paragraphs   Grades 2–3
• challenging vocabulary • short paragraphs • exciting stories
For newly independent readers who read simple sentences with confidence.

Ready for Chapters   Grades 2–4
• chapters • longer paragraphs • full-color art
For children who want to take the plunge into chapter books but still like colorful pictures.

STEP INTO READING® is designed to give every child a successful reading experience. The grade levels are only guides. Children can progress through the steps at their own speed, developing confidence in their reading, no matter what their grade.

Remember, a lifetime love of reading starts with a single step!

To Daddy, Mom, and Lisa, thanks for everything.

Text and illustrations copyright © 2001 by Antonia Zehler. All rights reserved under International and Pan-American Copyright Conventions. Published in the United States by Random House Children's Books, a division of Random House, Inc., New York, and simultaneously in Canada by Random House of Canada Limited, Toronto.

www.stepintoreading.com

Educators and librarians, for a variety of teaching tools, visit us at www.randomhouse.com/teachers

Library of Congress Cataloging-in-Publication Data
Zehler, Antonia.
Two fine ladies have a tiff / by Antonia Zehler. p. cm. — (Step into reading. A step 2 book)
SUMMARY: Two refined lady friends have a very unrefined disagreement.
ISBN 0-375-81104-4 (pbk.) — ISBN 0-375-91104-9 (lib. bdg.)
[1. Friendship—Fiction. 2. Conflict management—Fiction.]
I. Title. II. Series: Step into reading. Step 2 book. PZ7.Z36 Tw 2003 [Fic]—dc21
2002014890

Printed in the United States of America 12 11 10 9 8 7 6 5 4 3

STEP INTO READING®

STEP 2

Two Fine Ladies Have a Tiff

By Antonia Zehler

Random House 🏠 New York

Two fine ladies
woke up one day.
One of them yawned.
The other one frowned.

"Cover your mouth
when you yawn,"
said the fine lady
with the frown.

"It's not polite to point,"
said the first fine lady.
"Pooh," said the other.

They ate breakfast.
They were <u>not</u> polite.
"Elbows should not
be on the table,"
said one.

"Thbbbt,"
said the other.

They got dressed.

"That is not
your color,"
said one.

"Those are
my beads,"
said the first.

"Are not,"
said the other.

"Are so,"

said one.

"Are not!"

said the other.

Oh no!

The beads broke!

One fine lady

began to cry.

She put on
her coat.
"I am leaving,"
she said.

She went outside.

The other fine lady said,
"Good! I will spend
the day alone."

One lone fine lady
made some tea.

It was not the same
without the
other fine lady.

She looked out
the window.

The other fine lady

was on the porch.

She looked very sad.

One fine lady
picked up the beads.

She strung them
back together.

She put on
her coat

and went outside.

"For you,"
said one fine lady
to another.

The other fine lady
smiled.
"Thank you,"
she said.

"You're welcome.
Would you like
some tea?"

The answer was
yes.